VOL 1: CHASE THE CROWN

STORY AND ART BY
INUUPEN

CAVE KING

VOL 01: CHASE THE CROWN

STORY AND ART BY
INUUPEN

SHRINE COMICS Editorial
Jin Chan Yum Wai
DeAndre Moffett
Bree
Christian Sandino
Martin "Dragonniar" Brüsin

Lettering
Mohamed Reda
Jin Chan Yum Wai

Printed in China

Published by SHRINE COMICS

ISBN 978-0-6483217-5-0

CONTENTS

HURRY! GET TO THE ADVENTURE ALREADY! START READING!!

Minea Orphanage

ALRIGHT, SETTLE DOWN EVERY- ONE!

CHAPTER 0: ON THAT DAY...

REMEMBER, YOUR CAREER PATH SHEETS ARE DUE BY THE END OF THE WEEK!

I'M LOOKING FORWARD TO SEEING WHAT ALL OF YOU ASPIRE TO BE!

WHAT DID YOU PUT DOWN?

I'M GONNA BE A MINER! WHAT ABOUT YOU?

I'M GONNA JOIN THE MANA POLICE! PRETTY COOL, HUH?

HA! HA! HA! HA! HA! HA! HA! HA! HA!

HUH? SOMETHING FUNNY, LUCAS?

THE MANA POLICE AND MINERS SOUND COOL AND ALL, BUT I'VE GOT BIGGER DREAMS!

HAVE A SEAT, LUCAS.

I BELIEVE YOU AND I NEED TO HAVE A PRIVATE DISCUSSION.

AS IF!

LIKE I'D WANNA DO THAT CRAP FOR THE REST OF MY LIFE.

COME ON, HURRY UP! OR WE'LL MISS HIM!

I'M GOING AS FAST AS I CAN!

WHAT'S UP WITH YOU GUYS?

YOU DIDN'T HEAR?

BIG BRO REX IS BACK!!

AH, THAT'S RIGHT. THERE WERE TEN OF US THAT LEFT TO BECOME SPELUNKERS, WEREN'T THERE?

YEAH! YOU GUYS SAID YOU'D CREATE ONE OF THE BEST SPELUNKING GUILDS IN THE WORLD!

YEAH...

SO, HOW IS IT? I BET BEING THE LEADER OF A TOP GUILD IS HARD!

THAT'S WHY YOU GUYS DON'T VISIT OFTEN, RIGHT?

THERE
IS NO
GUILD...

HUH?

...YOU
MEAN

FWOOSH!!
THEY KNEW WHAT THEY WERE SIGNING UP FOR WHEN THEY BECAME SPELUNKERS.
...AT THE END OF THE DAY, THEY WANTED TO GRASP EVERYTHING LIFE HAD TO OFFER.
BAM!!
ALL LIFE HAD TO OFFER? YOU'RE TALKING ABOUT IT AS IF IT'S SOME TREASURE YOU CAN HOLD!
HEH.
PERHAPS.
WAIT... IS IT!?
GAAH!!
I DON'T KNOW, MAN, IT'S KINDA HARD TALKING TO A KID WITH SNOT ALL OVER THEIR FACE...
STEP
I'M NO KID, I'LL WIPE IT ALL OFF!!
STEP

WAIT, I NEED TO KNOW!! ARE YOU SAYING THAT—

EXCUSE ME! YOU'RE NOT THE ONLY ONE THAT WANTS TO TALK WITH BIG BRO REX, LUCAS!

HA HA!

YOU GUYS HAVE GOTTEN BIG TOO!

GUESS YOU'RE NOT MISSING ANY MEALS!

IS HE CALLING ME FAT?

DO—ZOH.

HEY, MOM... I'M HOME.

AND THE OTHERS?

WELCOME HOME...

MY FOOLISH SON!

RING! RING!

SORRY, GOTTA TAKE THIS.

WHAT'S UP?

...THE TRIGGER?

SORRY, I THOUGHT I'D BE ABLE TO STAY A FEW DAYS, BUT THIS IS URGENT.

WHAT!?

BUT WE DIDN'T EVEN GET TO CATCH UP! LUCAS, YOU'RE SO SELFISH!!

HOW'S IT MY FAULT!

IF IT MEANS ANYTHING, I HAVE SOMETHING IMPORTANT TO TELL YOU THREE.

FOLLOW ME!

AND MOM...

JUST GO. EVEN IF I TOLD YOU TO STAY, YOU'D STILL GO.

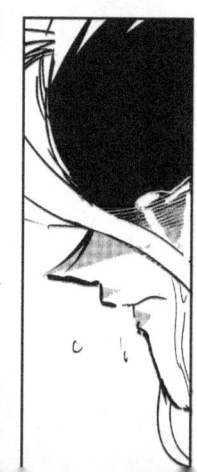

MYSTERIOUS CAVE DUNGEONS ARISE RANDOMLY ALL OVER ATLUS.

THEY HOLD SCARCE MAGICAL METALS THAT ARE CAPABLE OF THINGS WE STILL CANNOT FATHOM.

GUARDED BY VICIOUS MONSTERS...

AND SAVAGE BEASTS.

DESPITE THESE DANGERS, WE SPELUNKERS CONTINUE TO CLIMB ATLUS, CHASING THE CROWN JEWEL...

THE MYTHICAL STONE SAID TO BE CAPABLE OF GRANTING ANY WISH IMAGINABLE.

LOCATED
IN THE PALM OF ATLUS, HE
PROTECTED THE CROWN JEWEL
WITH HIS VERY LIFE.

IT'S SAID THE ONE WHO FINDS THEMSELVES TO BE THE CAPTOR OF THE CROWN JEWEL...

WILL BE CROWNED THE CAVE KING!

WOW!

COOL.

AWESOME!

I'LL DO IT! I'LL BE THE ONE TO REACH THE PALM OF ATLUS!

AND I'LL REACH IT BEFORE YOU, REX!

THIS IS THE STORY ALL SPELUNKERS ARE TOLD WHEN BEING RECRUITED INTO THE CAVE CORPORATION!

I FIGURED YOU'D SAY THAT.

YOU HAVE THE FIRST QUALITY EVERY SPELUNKER NEEDS... DRIVE!

BUT IF YOU WANNA BECOME THE CAVE KING BEFORE ME, YOU'RE GONNA NEED FUEL FOR THAT DRIVE, AND RIGHT NOW THAT'S WHAT YOU'RE LACKING!

THERE ARE MILLIONS OF DUNGEONS AND BILLIONS OF MONSTERS. EVEN THE BEST SPELUNKERS STILL LACK THE THREE FUNDAMENTALS OF SPELUNKING.

IT TAKES COURAGE...

...GRIT...

...AND LUCK!

TO HAVE WHAT IT TAKES TO BE...

CHAPTER 1: THE ZODIAC TRIGGER

Minea
Orphanage

HA
HA
HA

COOL!

DARN
IT.

AAAAH!!!

EXCUSE
ME.

MISS
DORMIR,
PLEASE TAKE
YOUR PROBLEM
BACK.

LUCAS
AGAIN?
REALLY?!

HEY,
WATCH IT,
YOU!

FIRST THINGS FIRST, WE WAIT UNTIL LUNCHTIME, THAT WAY MOM HAS TO BE IN THE HOUSE WITH ALL THE OTHER KIDS.

NEXT, WE SNEAK TO THE SOUTH GUARD POST.

AND CLARISSA DISTRACTS HIM.

WAIT, WHY DO I HAVE TO BE THE DISTRACTION?!

FINE, DK, YOU DISTRACT HIM!

UHH... SURE!

WHILE YOU DISTRACT HIM...

I'LL USE ONE OF THESE!

[SNOOZITE]

A CHROMA METAL THAT RELEASES SLEEP-INDUCING PARTICLES, HIGHLY SOUGHT AFTER FOR CRAFTING ENCHANTED ARTIFACTS. LEGENDS SPEAK OF ITS MESMERIZING POWERS, OFFERING A SERENE ESCAPE INTO THE REALM OF DREAMS.

UH... DID WE KILL HIM?

WOOOOOH!!

GOD NO, DK, ARE YOU CRAZY?!

HE'S SNORING, THE BALL FORCED THE SNOOZITE TO WORK!!

HA HA HA HA HA

LUCAS, THIS ISN'T FUNNY, WE'RE GOING TO BE GROUNDED FOREVER BECAUSE OF YOU!

LET'S JUST GO TELL MOM AND MAKE THIS A LIGHTER PUNISH-MENT!

WHAT ABOUT MY BALL?!

WE HAVE NO CHOICE!

TOSS!

WE AT LEAST GOTTA GET DENKA'S BALL!

SERIOUSLY! I CAN'T GO BACK WITHOUT MY LUCKY BALL.

Minea Village Outskirts
Crystal Cove
ADVENTURE! ADVENTURE! ADVENTURE!
WAIT UP, LUCAS!!

HURRY UP, ADVENTURE AWAITS!

WHAT THE HECK IS THAT?!

HAHA!! IT LOOKS KINDA LIKE THE VILLAGE GUARD!!

GROSS.

ALRIGHT GUYS! LET'S CONTINUE OUR ADVENTURE! THE FIRST ONE TO FIND TREASURE, WINS!

NO, LUCAS! WE ARE ONLY HERE FOR THE BASEBALL!

ERR, RIGHT, THE BASEBALL IS THE TREASURE!!

NOW LET'S EXPLORE EVERYWHERE UNTIL WE FIND IT!

NO "TREASURE," ONLY THE BASEBALL, NOW GET MOVING!!

WHAJU YOMEAN? (WHAT DO YOU MEAN?)
WE HAVE THE PRIME MINISTER OF CAVE CORP. BREATHING DOWN OUR NECKS, BOULDER.
VILLAGE
YOU'VE GOT TO START TAKING THIS SERIOUSLY...
...OR WE'LL BOTH BE WITHOUT A JOB.
NEWS FLASH, "MR. FAMOUS OF THE KINGDOM," EVERYONE WANTS TO BE PICKED BY YOU, YET YOU TURN THEM ALL DOWN. CAN'T YOU JUST SELECT AT LEAST ONE PERSON?!
SLAM!!
WE HAVE UNTIL THE END OF THE MONTH TO HAVE THE PROPER NUMBER OF REGISTERED GUILD MEMBERS...
...OR HE SHUTS US DOWN, AND WE HAVE TO FIND WORK ELSEWHERE!

WELL, YOU KNOW WHAT TIME IT IS!
DON'T EVEN SAY IT.
TIME FOR ADVEN-TURE!
NO WAY! IF WE GO HOME NOW, WE MIGHT NOT GET CAUGHT.
ADVENTURE! ADVENTURE! ADVENTURE!
BUT CLARISSA! WHAT ABOUT DK'S BALL? WE CAN'T JUST LEAVE IT BEHIND, WE'RE ALREADY HERE!
FORGET IT! WHAT PART OF "NOT GETTING CAUGHT" DON'T YOU UNDER-STAND?!
VRM VRM VRM
UH, GUYS, THE DUNGEON IS DOING SOMETHING WEIRD.

WE'RE INSIDE OF AN ACTUAL DUNGEON!!

WOOO HOO!! NOW WE CAN REALLY BECOME SPELUNKERS! LET'S FIND SOME TREASURE!!

SPELUNKER MY BUTT, YOU AND DK CAN GET LOST. I'M STAYING RIGHT HERE!!

GUYS, I THINK WE SHOULD STICK TOGETHER.

BESIDES, I-IT COULD GET DANGEROUS RIGHT, C-CLARISSA?

HUP.

HOLY CRAP! HOLY CRAP! HOLY CRAP! DENKA, CHECK THIS OUT!!

IT'S TREASURE!!

REALLY?!

WE'RE GONNA BE SPELUNKERS!!

YA SEE IT?

YEAH, YOU THINK IT COULD BE A TRAP?

MAYBE WE SHOULD WAIT FOR HELP, JUST TO BE SAFE!

WHY? SO THEY CAN TAKE THE TREASURE WE FOUND?!

NO WAY!

SURE, THEY'RE WEIRD LOOKIN' BUT I DON'T THINK THEY'RE EVIL!

SEE?! ONLY SOMETHING EVIL WOULD CHASE US DOWN LIKE THIS, IT'S TOTALLY OUT TO KILL US!

WELL, I MEAN WE ARE IN ITS "HOUSE" AFTER ALL.

A DEAD END?!

K'A BOOM

WAIT, YOU'RE NOT THINKING OF JUMPING, ARE YOU?!

WHAT OTHER CHOICE DO WE HAVE?!

CRUMBLE

CRUMBLE

CRAP!

WA... WAIT! LET'S JUST, UH... APOLOGIZE OR SOMETHING!

I'LL TAKE MY CHANCES JUMPING!

...IT'S TIME FOR ADVENTURE!!

FIRST THINGS FIRST! WE GOTTA FIND A WAY OUTTA HERE!

AND FAST, THIS PLACE IS GIVING ME THE CREEPS!

WAIT, THAT SLIME'S ASLEEP?!

ALRIGHT! NEXT STOP IS WHEREVER CLARISSA IS!

SEE YA, SLIME BUDDY! REST UP!

YOU DESERVE IT, PAL!

LOOKS LIKE WE FOUND OUR EXIT!

WHAAAAAAT?! A MINE CART?! NO WAY!

WE CAN EXPLORE SO MUCH FASTER WITH THIS!

TA DA!

RIGHT?! I'M JUST GLAD WE DON'T HAVE TO WALK!

WAIT, ARE THOSE B-BATS?!

...HEY, AREN'T THEY SUPPOSED TO ATTACK US?!

WHY WOULD YOU WANT THAT?!

IT'S WEIRD...

...ALMOST SEEMS LIKE THEY'RE RUNNING FROM SOMETHING.

WELL YEAH! JUST THINK ABOUT IT, WE LOOK LIKE TRUE SPELUNKERS TO THEM!

WHAT'S THAT SUPPOSED TO MEAN?!

MAYBE BECAUSE I TOUCHED IT FIRST, THERE'S A BOND!

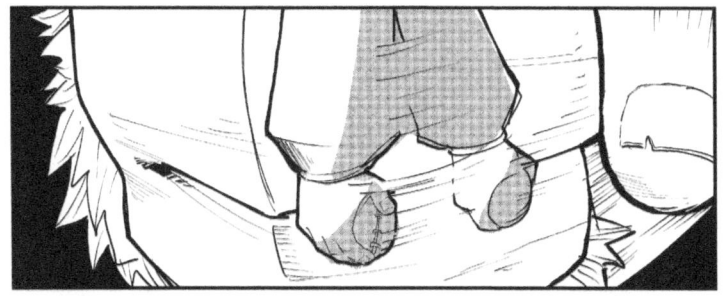

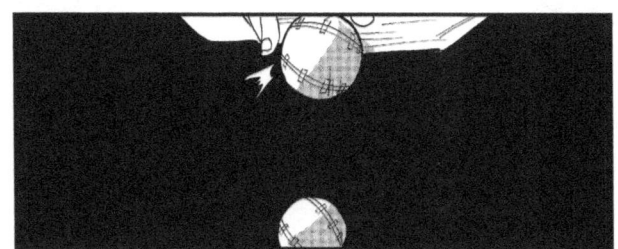

THE SYMBOL
FROM EARLIER...

THE
MONKEY...

THE SOUL AND CHROMA METALS GO HAND IN HAND.

THE BETTER YOU CAN CONTROL YOUR SOUL AND EMOTIONS...

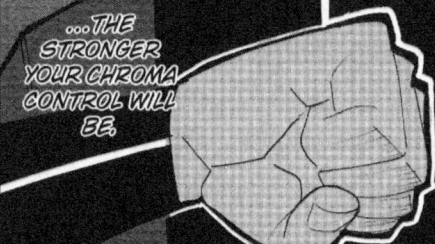

...THE STRONGER YOUR CHROMA CONTROL WILL BE.

THIS TECHNIQUE IS COMMONLY CALLED...

"ANIMA."

"THE WEAPON OF THE SOUL."

YOUR ANIMA CAN BE ANYTHING. A SWORD, GUN, OR AXE MAYBE EVEN THE MOST UNCONVENTIONAL OF OBJECTS LIKE...

DENKA'S...

BASEBALL!

IT ALL DEPENDS ON WHAT THE SPELUNKER'S SOUL TREASURES THE MOST!

I'LL NEVER FORGIVE YOU!

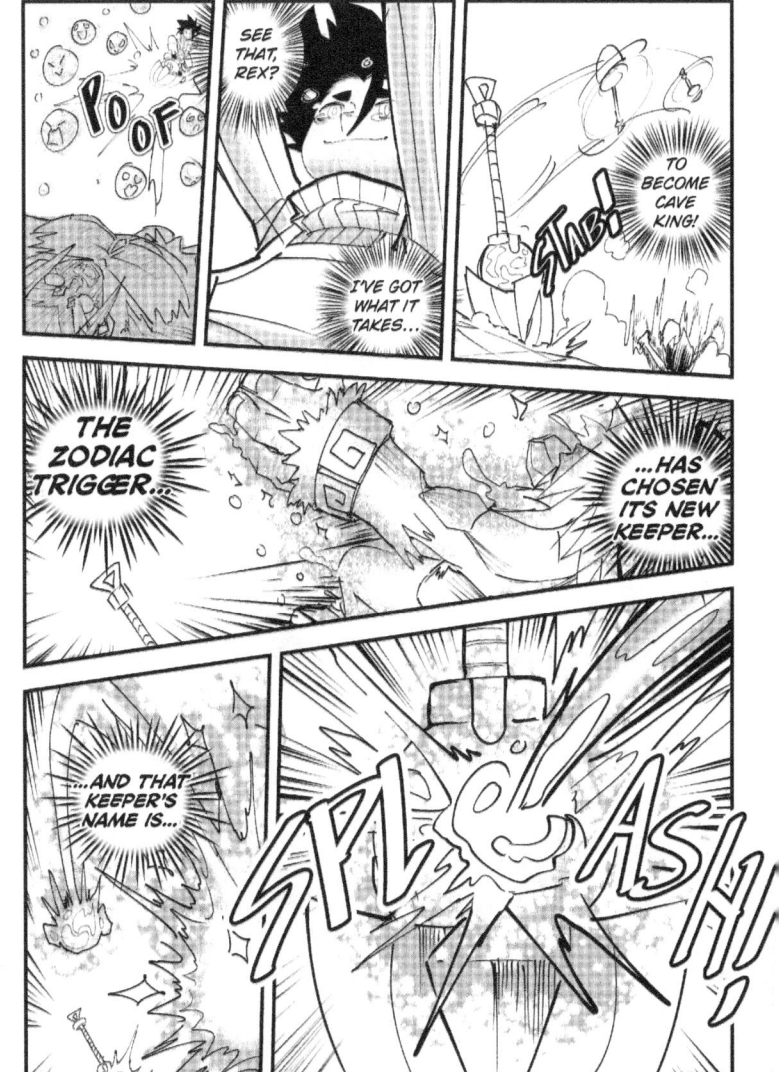

"THE ROCK"

CHAPTER 2: DEPARTURE

THESE ARE MINEA STONES.

MOM SAYS WHEN PEOPLE WEAR A FRAGMENT OF THE SAME ORE AS JEWELRY,

NO MATTER HOW FAR APART WE ARE, THESE STONES WILL LEAD US BACK TO EACH OTHER ONE DAY.

MOM STILL HAD TO HELP ME FORGE THEM...

BUT FEELING USEFUL, EVEN IF IT'S FOR SOMETHING LIKE THIS, IS ENOUGH.

AND THIS WAY I CAN BE WITH YOU GUYS IN SPIRIT!

NO MATTER HOW FAR YOU GO.
I'LL LOVE YOU BOYS...
FOREVER.
DO-DON!!
DON'T WORRY, MOM, CLARISSA!
WE'LL BE OKAY!

CHAPTER 3: EMBRACE YOUR DREAMS!

THESE THREE MUST BE IMPRESSIVE. NOT MANY TRAINEES CAN FIND "ROCK'N RAID HQ" ALONE IN THIS A-RANK DUNGEON ZONE...

HEY DUDE, BREATHE! THE HARD PART'S OVER.

D-DON'T WORRY, I-I'M FINE...

...LET ALONE MAKE IT UP THESE FLIGHTS OF STAIRS.

DON'T LIE TO HIM. IF A SIMPLE FLIGHT OF STAIRS CAUSED THIS MUCH FATIGUE, HE'S DONE FOR.

YOU'RE BETTER OFF GOING BACK HOME. THE HARD PART'S JUST BEGUN.

YET, HE MADE IT UP THE STAIRS.

SO WHAT'S YOUR POINT?

DO

YOU TWO CLOWNS SHOULDN'T EVEN BE NEAR A DIAMOND RANK DOJO.

DON!

WHAT WAS THAT?

YOU HEARD ME.

PEOPLE WHO CAN'T MIND THEIR BUSINESS END UP IN TROUBLE.

TROUBLE? DON'T MAKE ME LAUGH.

NOTHING'S FUNNY ABOUT THE EFFORT OF SOMEONE TRYING TO REACH THE SAME GOAL.

TAK!

TAK!

THERE'S NO WAY YOU'D CALL CLIMBING A STAIRCASE EFFORT!

EVERY STEP TO GET HERE WAS EFFORT IN MY EYES.

EFFORT ISN'T REWARDED AFTER EVERY MINOR ACCOMPLISHMENT. IF HE'S WHEEZING RIGHT NOW, HE'LL BE DEAD LATER.

AN ATTORNEY, ALSO CALLED A LAWYER, PROVIDES CLIENTS WITH LEGAL ADVICE AND REPRESENTS THEM AND THEIR LEGAL RIGHTS IN BOTH CRIMINAL AND CIVIL CASES.

THIS CAN BEGIN WITH IMPARTING ADVICE, THEN PROCEED WITH PREPARING DOCUMENTS AND PLEADINGS, AND SOMETIMES ULTIMATELY, APPEARING IN COURT TO ADVOCATE ON BEHALF OF CLIENTS.

TO PROTECT AND SERVE, MUCH LIKE DANGO, MY MOTIVATION COMES FROM MY FATHER. HE WAS A HERO DEFENDING THE INNOCENT IN A CORRUPT SYSTEM.

BEFORE I KNEW IT, MY FATHER VANISHED WITHOUT A TRACE AND WAS LATER CONFIRMED DECEASED.

THE ONLY THING I HAVE LEFT OF HIM IS THIS BOOK OF LAW.

IT'S FINE, YOU ALL HAVE YOUR REASONS FOR BEING HERE.

SOME BIG, SOME SMALL, BUT THEY ALL MATTER.

GRRR!

HMPH!

AS LONG AS YOU HAVE A REASON THAT YOU'RE PROUD OF...

THAT'S ENOUGH FOR ME, SO BEOWULF, STARTING NOW...

NEVER HESITATE TO SHARE YOUR DREAMS, EMBRACE THEM PROUDLY!

NEXT VOLUME

LUCAS VS BEOWULF!!

WHO DESERVES THE THROWN?!!

INUUPEN
KAMYRIN M. IRBY

Hey there! Thanks for picking up this volume (something I never thought I'd have!). This series is a love letter to everything my childhood self adored growing up. I appreciate all of you spending your hard-earned money on this (even though the content is free). I'll make sure the story of Cave King is one you'll remember!

P.S. This picture was taken on Christmas of 2021. Despite the tough times during COVID, many amazing opportunities came my way that I'm still so grateful for. This Christmas is one for the books!

Extra:
Dango's Exhaustion

AQUADITE

SNOOZITE

"MINEA STONE"

CHROMIUM

Lucas

D.K

Clarissa